CW00552110

THE ILLUMINATED WORLD

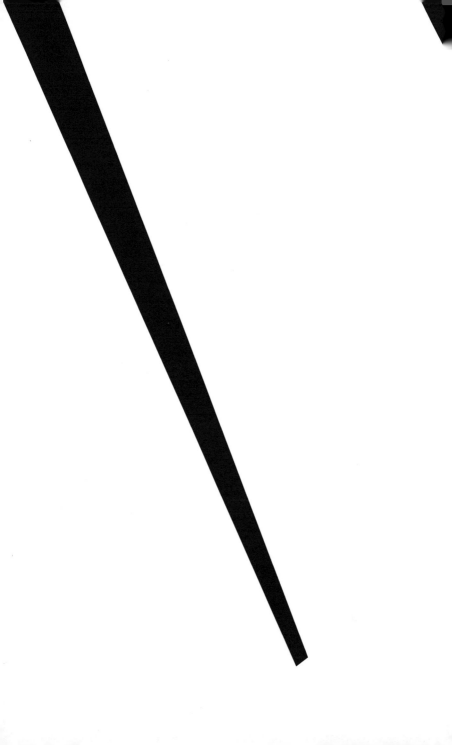

EYEWEAR PUBLISHING

JEMMA BORG
THE
ILLUMINATED
WORLD

First published in 2014
by Eyewear Publishing Ltd
74 Leith Mansions, Grantully Road
London w9 1lj
United Kingdom

Typeset with graphic design by Edwin Smet
Author photograph Anne-Sophie Olive
Printed in England by TJ International Ltd, Padstow, Cornwall

The right of Jemma Borg to be identified as author of
this work has been asserted in accordance with section 77
of the Copyright, Designs and Patents Act 1988
ISBN 978-1-908998-26-2

WWW.EYEWEARPUBLISHING.COM

'For I am every dead thing,
In whom love wrought new Alchimie'

John Donne

Jemma Borg was born in Essex.
She took a first in zoology at Oxford, where
she also completed a doctorate in evolutionary
genetics. She has worked as a science editor,
environmental campaigner and teacher and has
travelled and lived in places including Australia,
Pakistan and Hong Kong. Her poems have been
widely published in magazines and anthologies
and she has received prizes including the
New Writing Ventures Award for Poetry in
2007 and a residency at the Leighton
Artists' Colony at the Banff Centre
in Canada in 2009. She currently
lives in East Sussex with her
husband and young son.

Table of Contents

How it is with the circle

Actually it's just a line, but all points
are equidistant from the centre without
distortion and that's what makes it special.
Contained by and within that line are all
the attributes of circularity: the infinite
exactitude of π, a disc too correct
to be a moon or an eye, though sure enough
to be a wheel, a curve that is not
a skull or a country's anxious border,
but that untroubled arc the compasses draw:
the black lead circle, stark and unbreached.

But we haven't come nearly far enough.
What does a circle become if you puncture it?
All lines and roads and scars. Did Euclid
consider this? Arcs rejoining to make circlets,
their untethered balloons, for a moment,
carrying rainbows, as soap bubbles do.
And the insides – all that was circle –
seeping out into the circumambient air.
What of desire? The body is drawn
towards the shape of its perfect star:
to be something else, to be something more.

The mathematician

From his window, he could see snow falling as the fractals
he couldn't see but which he relied on being there.

There were numbers lost at the end of his imagination
like countries so far away he'd never make it to them.

A shadow fell and then he heard a crack as of glass:
below, against the conservatory, an icicle

like an organ pipe or stalactite of diamond
had shattered into its pieces of supercooled clarity.

He thought of her skin: it was as seductive of light
as ice. It was impossible to talk to her.

On a sheet of paper, he began a series of equations:
numbers teaming up as water does, irresistible to itself

in the cold, numbers aligning like the tracks of a sledge
in unmeeting parallel. Then they writhed like meltwater.

He held a set of keys for locks that may not exist.
Or was he shadowing the word that set the world ringing?

The dusk was growing deeper. Houses on the other side
of the horizon began switching on their lights

and he also reached for his lamp. There were some things
of which he could be certain. The rest was love.

A short treatise on a squid

Overhead, yes, the shark hangs
like a Renaissance saint, in whose eyes time
falls like a sediment, and no doubt
the machinations of a moray eel's jaws
are more dangerous than teeth in a glass
and it is not grief that makes the upward,
filling mass of little bells – the jellyfish –
drop again as a heart does into sorrow,
but it's in the basement's deep and damp Atlantic,
among the transparent skins of fish
and the skeletons worn with a monstrous clarity,
that the greatest exaggeration is made
as *Vampyroteuthis infernalis* heaves into view.

That name. It reminds me of Prudentius
who said the corruption of language
is at the root of sin. Once Satan's tongue was split,
object and name slid off one another
like function and form in a tumour
or lovers making and remaking their union,
but still remaining alone. What crosses
the divide is not itself, but what has found
itself in another: an ecstasy of mind
where *like* is *like* is *like*... Dear metaphor
– read 'lover' – we invented heaven,
imagining sky as a fish might the land:
alien, beautiful on our tongue.

Chromatography

If it could, it would smell of lilacs.
If it could, it would rub its whiskered chin of violets.

It is the shade of a bruise and the gleam of aubergine
and the skin of plums
which hang their mouth-watering opulence
       in a haze of wasps.

Just there, disappearing if you look directly,
at the edges of a rainbow, it sublimes
       into grey slate clouds.

Ophelia made garlands with it
among the weeds that were growing by the stream

and the children of emperors were born into it
at the roots of a porphyry wall.

       A distant star shifts
its note into red as it speeds into the past;
what's coming towards us is blue.

At the crossroads of these two colours,
       the still moment waits.

You love that dark heart of its indifference.

If it could, it would taste of honey.
If it could, it would wear robes of roses.

It would not be itself at all.

Ghazal

Like clouds in a savannah sky, sleep passes
across the zoo's many eyes, its breathing pelts.

Some sleep with their eyes open –
like the crocodile in its dinosaur skin.

Some eyes glisten like freshly laid eggs,
and some are born blind and skin-raw as worms.

From birth, an elephant's skin is wrinkled,
its feet half-moons rising over mud.

The gorilla holds his old man's wisdom
in his hands, in his dried-riverbed skin.

Fish scales drop into a clear-watered dream;
a pearl glints in an opened shell.

Don't jemmy me out from my skin: under its enclosure,
I'm waiting to tell you everything I've seen.

The cave's art

I wake to the undoing of morning,
             light angled without compromise
around the blinds onto a half-filled glass.

I descend into the mirror, then reveal the day
             as though uncovering a face
hidden by a sheet. Outside, the Vézère glitters

under the canoeist's oar, the trees on the bank
             duplicating themselves a little more
inaccurately. At Pech Merle, the prints on limestone

are all of right hands; at its deepest wall,
             where at Lascaux a horse is tumbling into
the abyss, women-shapes fuse with bison,

             a man grows the head of a bird.

                              ★

Beneath our torch, the rock comes alive with shapes
             it began, then we complete: the spine
of a bull, forelimbs of a deer, leg on leg

of correct perspective. My ancestors –
             whose mind is my own, the same self-
intensifying shadow – what in the world glows

so you may touch it? Each palm haloed in ochre
        is a silence. Around us, there is only
the permanence of flux, the slow muscling

of the stalactites' haunches and each life
        of yours reaching back and back, hand
over hand, until what we have called human

        closes again into its secretive bud.

★

There is nothing that is not us. The almost-
        chapel of the grotto, its growing tissues
of calcite, the inhabited architecture

of its natural basilica, the dome
        of dripping concentric sounds: not heaven
marking its image on earth, but what eyes make

of the forms of blindness: a union
        of soul and stone. It will be the same
with marble, and what is the weight and grain

of marble is not clearest in the quarry
        – not in that wound – but in the temples
the mind will come to make, so as to cover

        the wild rose of its loneliness.

Soul sends a letter at last

Ah, you should see the light in Alexandria,
above the harbour, in the hour before noon.
I arrived here on Wednesday by train from Cairo,
the seats very generous in first class.

For a while, I was unsure of who I was
– the heat can be disconcerting –
and even a dirty sea would have been welcome,
although that was not what I found.

Everything in the Sahara had been one colour:
the camels, the giant bricks of the pyramids.
It's only the sky that orientates you.
The ascent into the belly of the great Khufu

to the small space they called 'tomb' –
but where no king's swaddled body was ever found –
was just as unnerving: did I travel to the stars
or burrow down into the earth?

Neither head nor feet would have settled
the matter: the lamps shone dimly in the shaft.
And, yes, I am sorry you have waited so long
for this letter to land at your door, but this

is the way we become aware of each detail
of our separation, and it's only at night
we miss one another, my dear. In the day,
I must confess, I barely remember your name.

The caryatids

On Athena's sacred hill, the caryatids
        are losing the curl from their hair.
Their intention is to float –
        radical, their sense of themselves –

but the melodious principles that raised them
        did not make them free
and into the drama of their vertical dimension,
        there is a crumbling away.

Suffers and suffers the bright world
        they say as they decline,
stoic as maps, though they still balance
        on their heads, like women carrying water,

the weight of their suffering.
        Should they fall, as they must,
they will sleep like the gods, the sky overhead
        shifting blues through its hourglass.

No dreams for those with wildflowers
        in their hair: their lucid spines will crack
with the weight of the unmade world,
        a world they once raised in their arms.

The Pond

Your *perhaps* stands astride two worlds, two
sentences: I rest on its minor colossus
as you do on that image of twilight, both glad
for it and wishing, instead, to see more clearly.
When you're late, as you are now, I take out
your letters and read their slow anachronism,
their tentative words, midsummer-born.

You once messaged to ask if I was real.
Remember the Heath, I laughed. That afternoon:
you swimming in the cool and me watching.
The water was heavy, dark, but your head glided
smoothly – into shade, into light, into shade –
like a book opening up its fan in the breeze
and words seen, not seen, then seen again.

Which is it you prefer: the summer we shared
where the light was tempered by oak leaves,
the smell of closely shorn grass and the quiet
of women drying themselves on the verge,
or your tropical sun which leaves no bareness
unturned? You carry lateness rather than decide.
Meanwhile, the hours I wait are growing.

Like water reflected on the banks of the pond,
something keeps moving and making me turn
around to see who walks towards me,
but never arrives. Each time, it's only the trees
shifting. So, waiting becomes this finer state
that grows a form from the wavering of light
and sets me still – like a deer – listening.

Relic

Bell Laboratories, New Jersey, 1965

One whole year on our hands and knees,
clearing pigeons from the curious ear
of the antenna, listening for silence

under the city's noise and the pulsar's roar
and still this sound as weather makes at a door,
a low worry everywhere, burrowing

into the hours from the immovable darkness,
uncurling its strong horsehead,
until we catch it, finally, as a telescope does

in its wide dish, until we hear it
for what it is: this sound of creation
whose infinitesimal enormity

is now a thin travelling irritation;
this sound of time clocking on
        and now corroded into this radio hiss.

Nocturne

Then the Moon is a painful desert:
no heat or ice bruises and fractures the rock,
no overripe clouds pock its surface with hailstones.

This is what fell from our side: ocean floor, basalts and ash
sizzling, then reforming into this
bare and luminescent skull

over which the great mare, Earth, rises
          in signature.

★

Among solutions of rock and rubble,
iridescent planets riddled with sulphurous breath
and a dark in which nothing rattles,

there is this: our absurd realm
of hurricanes and lizards of mountain-spines
above which the stars

like thousands of enlightened souls
          are guttering and guttering
and our Earth's flowering in all its effervescence:

          brief, as all possible bliss is.

★

Look at Saturn! Falling like a pale apple
along the ecliptic's line: imperfect circle
orbited with ellipses, blue diamond in a ring.

Tilted by an hour, it drops – lens by lens –
to arrive at my eye and light, directly, my mind:
I see it! The distance between us is nothing!

I go to it as though I were shipwrecked
        and this my island.

But we are sinking, the Earth and I,
to the right, to the right, and drifting to the left
in the telescope's eye: this apparition, Saturn,

        unrooted in the night sky.

*

Midnight. And I wake to find nothing asleep.
The pods of last year's love-in-a-mist
open up, leaking their black moons,

and night-lovers – tobacco plants and jasmine –
wreak opulence on the dark,
        under the lit matches of stars.

The Earth seethes with moving mouths
and captured light alive in leaves.
In the garden, with the cold rising up through my feet,

what is it I'm enacting, moth-like, transient?
Life runs against the tide.
        It makes errors all the time.

Engines of the travelling earth

after Sam Taylor-Wood's 'Crying Men'

They each cry for the camera: some naked,
some hiding their faces with their hands

as if expecting a blow. Some look at us directly,
like this one here: a suspended angel, weeping

two long lizards of travelling rains,
two broken eggs, two glistening stories

of complaint and brilliance, his skin
a field of sympathetic forms – open, skewed,

then folding – his vulnerability
a fever of wounds. No one is intervening.

If we could, we'd look away from this
crowded room of men taking on their burden,

as they sit at windows, as they get out of bed.
We are brought to witness, not to rest, but to see

the delivery of pain, and to bear it
in ourselves, this grief that bends us as though

we were beings made of light. To see is to follow
the eye's translucent grief into the grief of stars.

The distances between us are growing.

An entry on flint—

        from rods of silica
and the spicules of sponges and the long-dead
in their grave-seams, the veins of flint were formed:
water into stone, in the sea-channels of the earth.

For the jewelled chalcedony of the black flint,
for the prize of its fractures, for its opalescent
edge that blunts more slowly than steel,
the Breckland heath was opened

to the mines' galleried dark, a trespass
the ancients amended with offerings of pots and shoes
and bodies of deer laid out along the main shafts.
The mines granted their dampness and gloss,

knuckles of flint fell out from the hammered walls.
From the dream in the mind, so to the hand:
an industry of axe-head then musket
across which the blood of enemies was drawn.

When the wars moved elsewhere
as the old weaponry died, only the bats remained
to spark the darkness with their wings.
The mines closed again with mouthfuls of grass

        and the flint bedded down
under the pastures like an army of bones.
When we dig, it is through seam on seam of ruin.
The flint-sheen rings into flooded fields.

As flamingos at the water's edge

After thirty years, I find I've come to the place
where sorrows grow. Here is the cataract
of the Salar de Uyuni, sun-encrusted
with gypsum's satin spar and desert rose,
here are the pins of jewellers' quartz
on which gold chains drape themselves
like idle iguanas, here is the debris born
from a glacier's boom and shattering decline.
Strange chemistries that tears perform:
falling from my eyes as glass, then gathering
at my feet in angles of brow and nose and mouth.
Where has tenderness gone? I ask the broken mirror.
Am I also a multitude of ghosts?
A sliver of its silvered edge enters my heel,
then travels the nerve to lodge its sharpness
behind my eyes and close them with tears:
these new tears, which fall as airships do
– in a slow, slow, infolding crash –
or as water does from a flamingo's throat
as it drinks from the lake's molten edge.
Salt, salt. Then an uprising of garish wings.

Drawing the ladder

If I look, there is no surface, no hinge,
no bracket or screw, no line of aluminium,
no striation to secure the foot, rung
by rung, no place the ladder gains the earth,
no place the floating weight lands, no full part
that is not obscured by shadows falling
from the pepper tree or by old, caked mud.
Up to the thin leaves, up to the adornment
of red peppercorns, there has been a year
of standing, a year of ghost foot on ghost foot
angled to the tree and climbing. As the storms
pass and the wind dies then rises, as the air
melts into an ancient insect busyness,
as the still nights of swallows and wine
ascend and decline: there has been this year
of slow non-decay, of infinite definition,
after which I come, with charcoal in hand,
and cannot make anything connect.

Can I only tell you about the rain?

'…making what comes next be
what we mean…'

Michael Donaghy

A downpour is a kind of comforting, I think.
Not a difficult thing: the thunderstorm on roofs and sills.
But these ceremonies break miserably
on the day: the rinsing, perpendicular rain
and the slow departure of the dead.

It had been that kind of season – months of rain
held down under a melancholic system:
death-knell of hurricane at our cold Atlantic door,
a deep enough pause to make memory shine.
I stood under the eaves of the house

and watched my tools being washed on the grass
and the bare, unplanted tree
and the rain that started as light
as spiders' feet, then found a heavier note
and a matching frame of mind.

Everything misses its mark, even grief.
So began my letters to the dead – to you, dear friend –
now you lay perfected under your sheet
and now you lay in the earth like a box of light
shut tight. I would take my share of you

and spread inaccuracy over you like melting wax.
As you might've said: *People are always unfinished.*
Or simply: *I died. It is very terminal.*

But the wordless senses continue to wander
through my mind for the root of something.

At first, I wrote as though you still suffered:
tell me, under the autumn,
                                    do you feel the rain on your eyes?
Then I stepped in with your reply:
I can't make myself heavier, dense again,
like a mountain and walk across to see you.

My legs no longer warm themselves
and this is a cold bed, alright, never relenting.
But the persistent rain is a wonderful friend,
with its thoughtful mourning.

Who was I to talk to you of the rain? The rain
meant nothing to you, and words are like that too:
they act only to verify our mourning,
sliding over things, caressing them,
                    but leaving them bare –

            words are for welcoming death.
I'd picked up a line of threads, but couldn't weave them.
It was worse than silence.
I couldn't name anything or know its material,
or meet the matter of an afternoon

with a constant sensation, whatever I summoned
missed its place – was more 'birds' than 'geese' –
and even this failure felt counterfeit,
not deep enough for grief.

Dear friend,
can we speak as we always did — one fiction to another?

While you made your funeral vows,
I was under a desert sky, near the tomb of Moses.
Or was it the resting place of his brother?
No one can tell: relics hide in a case,
          relying on an accumulation of faith.

And neither would you be conjured from your sanctuary.
The dead, they say, cannot be seen,
except by an averted gaze: slant on,
          like rain buffeted by wind,
I groped towards this puzzle set for the living.

But the rain's lesson was this: it does not speak,
its memories disappear, greedily, into the earth.
The rain is all throat, the word, the name
before it is spoken, the shape grief
sends out from the grey skies and the cold.

For now, dear friend, sink down into the welcoming earth:
          these are the difficult months.

I stood at the edge of the season.
Far below, my voice had spun and broken.
I listened for the words that would make their way back.

The rain does not construct false arguments
or ventriloquise the dead: it is a gesture of crossing
like a beacon-flare that leaps from peak to peak
or like you across the flaws of elegies
          to become nothing like yourself.

It was almost winter now: darkness lengthening
and the sky clear of migrations,
the geese far off, while the cold drew near.
I'd stared long enough into the darkness
            for what never seemed to come.

Grief requires the frame of sky to pull away
until the earth loses its blood, then its shadow.
It begins with the blistering rains, then the cold
climbs inside and breaks open pain

from its thundering rhyme. Only after a season
of vacancy can the land find its voice —
as I must too, until the oblivion has gone
and the earth that buried me roars.

To write to you, the effort of it, was to see the year turn.
I could almost believe the rain had written me:
in the small ruin of myself, the words came,
free as rain, falling through me
            in their continual disappearing act

and yet they stick. So the year would take me
and often I'd begin to write to you, then stop,
and sometimes the roar would blind me
and sometimes in the quiet I could hear
            the ripe machinery of grace.

To Hopkins' God

I do still think of you but the feeling is lean.
    The world cannot gather its grandeur and share
things with me, and I cannot feel my bare being
    or the spring or the westward-heading sun.
The ghosts of those who toiled with faith walk
    their silence through walls and into the night.
I used to think as they did, but that dream left
    nothing for this world. I will go to where
the soil is charged, in the east. There, the world
    is becoming *almost* and then actually *becoming*.
I will wake to the rain and my lover's back, and remember
    a love lower than the sky. It is a work of will,
but the world still shines: I see the bright-fantastic.
    You, however, have folded your wings, and decline.

Vow of silence

The mind, yes, the mind has mountains:
I grew them, hour by hour,
like layers of pearl.

Conscience – that sea –
is always raising its white-capped torments,
but I will not be wrecked in the storm.

The mouth of the sea
sighs all day long,
but the desert expects no lover.

I tell you, love is a prison
covered with the mouths of hunger.
This road here will take me to it.

The Way of the Cross

In the valley, a dog barks: its bark
becomes the valley. Then the man singing
outside the pastry shop: briefly, his voice

breathes the valley. The valley: bark and song.
Then silence or just the almost-heard
sound of heat rising up to the rocky peaks,

through the stiff yellow grasses, the stiff pine trees
shading the Stations of the Cross.
Each step takes me back on myself

and higher. The sounds to my left, then my right,
are voices in my head: I am heat,
and foot by foot on the path, I am the rustle of pines,

then song, then bark. Then fountain:
up by the chapel, water flows over a short fall of stones
and into a pipe hollowed in the valley's side.

In the chapel, behind the locked door,
the song and bark and gentle trickling are caught
at the corners of the roof and in the shadows.

When I first looked through the window sealed with wire,
I thought I saw a man standing on the altar.
When I looked again, I could see the falseness

of his skin, the slight fading of his plaster garments,
his stare of fire wrestling with a mountain.
Down in the valley of chime, where the sounds

wind into things again – the dog leashed on a rope,
the man bent to the road, with the song snagged
on the hillside like sheep hair – I come to

the roadside shrine where a star settles above
the immaculate child. There, where the persimmons grow,
a silence burns – silence deep as wine.

I am the sky over Malawi

and the rain conceals me in its shroud.
The ground is curved with backs and bellies,
an epidemic of eyes opened in the storm,

and the cattle shift their feet
and there is an incessant waiting.
I can hear moaning in the sound-shocked clouds,

in the grief-songs of each human mouth
but nothing where the soul used to hide –
only death, working its tendernesses

into the privacy of bone and the blood's glory.
At dawn, when a boy comes out to show me
his eyes – one dark as tea, the other

as uncomprehending as the blossoms
falling from the bougainvillea by the lake shore –
I do not look at him. I am the sky over Malawi

and the beautiful morning strikes my face.

A century of ravens in flight

'Why is our century worse than any other?'

Anna Akhmatova

You were right: it was a century of ravens
in flight, a thousand crosses revealing
nothing of the graves chalking the mud
in the intricacies of daylight, nothing

of the grief dividing the breathless black
of night or the stench of hair behind
the mirror's image. What was lost
would not rise again but in a stream of ashes.

The road took possession of the woods
like autumn and we drove its contortions
in the shining carapace of our car. At first,
we could still see the trees above us,

but then they became only spaces where light
was unable to pass. Ahead, a mouth of fire sank;
behind us, the fields were darkening.
Let nothing be forbidden, we said, then

plunged our fingers into the fabric
of our seats, our eyes in the rear-view mirror
partitioned from our faces. And still we drove
as though there was a spare world of air

we could reach on the westward route.
The corners of our minds that were sleeping, woke.
But the dawn would not break this night
nor do ravens sing and the ravens were in flight.

Modern fruit

I

The cherry ripens quickly:
it becomes soft and brown, then its skin splits
and the fungus takes off
like a white head of hair on end with static.
How sticky the bowl with its sugars!

However cool the bowl, the cherry will not last:
the decay is next to the china
and the cherries on top hide it beneath them
with an imperial gloss.

II

These hard nectarines, apparently already ripened red!
How illusory they are,
tucked under the honest, green-skinned bananas.
What explains such flushed cheeks?
Unripe and ripe, they look the same

though these will never share their beauty.
False witnesses, they preen in the shade.
No ode for you, little pharaohs:
you will go straight from lie to rot.

The decoration

The walls in the lounge have holes like bullet holes,
but our walls do not have bullet holes.
Over the hallway, the ceiling is down as though bombed,
but our ceilings are not bombed.
The bathroom plumbing is exposed like a wound
in the body, but our body has not been wounded.
You are not in the house or garden,
but you are not dead and your photo on the mantelpiece
is not a memorial. The war does not shake the foundations
of the house, but the house is shaking.
We are not committing acts of which we are ashamed,
but we are ashamed. We have no simple enemies.
What is done in our name is not done in our name
but sullies us, is ours, is ours like our name.

The orchard

'The morning by a tree of blood was dewed'
                    Federico García Lorca

In the orchard, *Malus* buds are thickening
with the troubled intentions of the apple.
The trees are as dark as coagulating blood.

What kind of malice is growing there?
A wound in which glass is embedded.

Twilight is moving slowly along the ground
like the ending of a fable
or the blood encircling the wound.

Everything falls to a centre. Everything falls:
the blood-rose, the stain of the rising sun,
the bare and contorted trees, their diagrams of bones.

In the dusk, a flush of bluebells is burning.
The earth is groaning in its bed.

And who is that riding out of the woods?
Only the moon, like a stone without a seed.

Bluebells

'That was the strange mine of souls.
As secret ores of silver they passed
like veins through its darkness'

                    Rainer Maria Rilke

I cannot say the strange mine of souls is empty.
Even in the depths of my sleep, in that muted calm,
I hear conspirators whispering like figures at the end
of a tunnel, planning to evict me from my life.
Or is it from my death? It can be difficult to tell.

I'd sought the darkness out and its echoless mirror,
I'd drunk it up, thirsty as litmus paper. And was it acid
or was it sweet? It's a distinction important to make,
as between *absence* and *emptiness*: while one grows
a return, the other cares only to fill its departure.

Each spring, when the sun opens the door
with bluebells, you reach out to grasp my hand
and pull me along the pale route into light: a routine
at which we stagger like mismatched dancers.
Stubborn lover you are, despite the blood on my lips.

But no more singing, no more high-pitched antics
or the minor wisdoms we find at the bottom of a glass.
The seasons may not last and I have towed out a thread
from my mind that leads to no aisle-lit exit sign.
I watch my life run on its spool and unwind.

This morning, as with any other, sleep pulls back
from the shore like a turning tide and the dead hour
passes in resuscitation, as the world is broken

by light. Slowly, I push the imprint of my face
upwards, like a narcissus ending its root-bound vigil.

And there is your hand on the pillow: quiet now,
with its five blind eyes, its five bitten nails.
What is it you awaken in the secrecy of our palms?
Do you remember the failures that live in the body's dream
or is it desire that wakes in the half-light?

Meditations on the apology

Even the woodworm are spies, with their rash
of eyes in the whirling grain of the floor.
There's nothing straight about this shame.

If I miss a note of the 'Moonlight Sonata',
it's not that I can't play it correctly,
it's just that the error was seductive.

Doesn't disease love a rose? Those anthers
like the antennae of moths, that fragrance
which enters through an open door...

The body is an ornament of error.
It corrupts a little more each day, like a word
whispered ear to ear and its spine softly ruined.

And what a small word *sorry* is: it soaks into our bed
like sweat and threads through the blind spot
of each eye with the tenor of its regret.

But how these eyes unfurl for you –
won't you lose yourself in their charms?
If you open the judgement, you can take out the gift.

The Long River

To the East China Sea, the Long River
drops and drains through Horse Lung
and Ox Liver, the narrow vertical limestone

it blasts then slaloms through
with its unfinished veins and sharp flowing
        hairpins, raising up coffins on the precipices

while the gorges breathe through each valve
green peaks and clouds, and its blue water
        fills up with mud through which the sturgeon

hauls an ever-fading presence, and then on, surging
past the banks of Golden Sands and rot,
        under the impossible bridges

        where the Russian barges perch
on its dangerous full stretch, past the empty villages
waiting to be flooded, to where it widens at last

        at the plug of dam and lock: not a weeping river
like the Yellow, which is called China's Sorrow,
but one with all its crying done in Sichuan

where, above the straining water, the mountains
        form a mother with her child – just there,
by Sword and Book – her song like a wire

through the wind's tributaries, her song
which is the river: the Long River, the Yangtze,
        city by city, slowly lowering its names.

The lover of Amazonian catfish

They say it's rational to turn inwards
to your obsession, to wake to it and love it,
but I tell you, when the storms come down
and the rain falls like stones onto the river,
I can't open my eyes to its sting.
      My childless hip

starts up its ache along the beltline
where I hook my thumb. Then the waves come
up over the canoe as if to drown me
within reach of shore, and I have to think
of where to jump to should a caiman
      land at my feet.

But it passes. And then, above the cataracts,
where the water eases and takes the rain
like a boiling mirror instead:
always a greater treasure of fish,
and then a greater one still in the tiny creeks
      we call *igarapés*

and into that slow-moving catch
as bizarre as a netted dream, I sink
my heart's current, the lines of its wonder
tracing the body of my fish
from the promontory of its ancient head
      to its long and breakable tail.

A strangely dressed murmur of water

appeared in my belly. 'My bones are still soft,'
it said. 'I remember them glinting
like obsidian in the rolling earth.'
                    It was stone that was its mother.

An arrow point flew into my belly
and wrote with its nib: 'Every season is the word *wait*,
bitter on the tongue.'
                    It would not call me mother.

A star fell like a pearl from a string
then settled, burning, in my lap: 'I seethe with gold,'
it said. 'My heart is made of iron.'
                    No lullaby could soothe its throat.

As the sun set, blood ran under the horizon
and spoke of the body it would make out of light:
the clockwork, fishtail and spine.
                    It said the westerly wind was its mother.

As I slept, the darkness bled into my eyes.
'See where I land,' that darkness said.
'There I grow roots, coronae and smoke.'
                    It was the seed that made the air choke.

At dawn, as horses of light came running,
my dandelion seed fell through the zero's O.
'Mother,' it said, 'I've left you a scent.'
                    It was like jasmine, only fainter in the dew.

'The mouth of love was empty: I could not drink.'

The sculpture

Since we've moved house, I've discovered
many things floating around us, organised
into circular layers as a mandala is, linking

our realm of suffering and the mundane
with its heaven. Right above our heads,
a TV's aura agitates the wall with its dramas,

then, like guardians against dissolution,
there are fabrics and quilts in layers
of silks and matts and all the off-colours:

Egyptian beige, paisley and flocked mint.
Then come the household goods, still sleeping
in their boxes, and a book that keeps opening up

to the same two-page spread: of chromosomes
dividing with the gesture of a parting kiss
and a frog transforming itself into a man

in twelve stages. From the ceiling, two bulbs
descend unshaded and naked as eggs
and an ammonite reflects its secretive coil

in a mirror by the bedroom door.
On our table, which seats 2 to 4,
there's a Thai wooden dragon, a dish of plums

with their two halves of unripened twins
and the frames in which our photos should lie,
displaying the darkness between limb and limb

of our pose. I'm waiting to fill one frame
with that picture of a sculpture I cut
from a magazine: standing on a white base,

raised by a black stem, it looks like two sponges
budding off one another in a light-filled room.
It makes me think I must work harder.

So, while you seem to have speed around you,
I have the near-emptiness of shelves
as though I had no past, just this one vase

stretched out into a tiny mouth. Now a face
appears like dust in the sun, and though symmetry
confers beauty, they say, this face

is unequal in joy and sorrow, and looks like neither
of us, though it is a union of ours
formed in the fused language of the unborn.

This solitary urchin – our sculpture – opens
its eyes like the seeds of a ripened fruit:
it's been learning the sounds of our join.

What beautiful risks are lost from each other,
it whispers, our little growing sunshine,
both banal and sublime, eating the power

of opposition and throwing out
its own strange light. Thus, from the fog: this fire.

A summer diary

'Woodman, cut off my shadow'

Federico García Lorca

Arrow to my heart, arrow to my belly,
the drug sounds its way
quietly, quietly through skin,

a small key to turn the rusting mechanisms
of my love! of my love! –
its locked cells, its hanging cities of bones,

the chamber of echoes where no flower blooms.
Those who will never be born – now,
they wake, like the sleeping dead stirring

under the sound of the horsemen and the horn,
devising fingers and toes
through an ontology of fish and toad.

They hear the sound of the key, they hear it
and rouse themselves: each bald head,
each wound-up coil and tail.

Waking is my unreasonable love, my wild love!
Waking are the unborn with their insatiable appetites.
More, they say. Always: *more*.

★

Among that host, I search for a face
as I had imagined it – my son, who arcs
into history like a shaft of light or Lorca's moon.

Let my belly receive that weight,
let its horizon settle and this one head rise
above the unborn – the one who was waiting

for this intersection: *here* and *now*.
You are my one sentence, one line, one word, I say,
that defends my obstinate centre from fear.

★

Elsewhere, the flowers thrive:
lupins with their swords of purple and red,
the foxgloves rising higher and higher –

each row of flowers that dies adding
to the next lengthening of their six-foot spines,
bees urgent at their cups of spotted leopards.

I grow larger, water's false pregnancy
pressing at my skin: I am tender
at each footfall, tender at each seating.

I hang my head under the scent of lilies
like a sick dog. A candle by the window
melts, then sets into a misshapen foot.

★

Twenty possible children drawn by needlepoint
now fall to thirteen in their dishes,
making their inconceivable union work.

By day five, only two remain, each a hundred
cells developing their complex intent.
Some eggs were drawn too early from their sleep

and others were as empty as husks, the seed
already scattered – I do not know where.
With breakfast, I am brought an egg cup

holding two *Dianthus*: two sweet williams
with a pinked margin. They make me cry:
I am so full, but it is not with grief. Something

is being born of which I must not speak,
as though it were the secret name of the soul.

★

On my bedrest, I watch the two lime trees
outside, shaking their green mass in the wind.
They are like islands of kelp

rising up through the sea. The world
has shrunk to the few steps I walk between bedroom
and bathroom, like a ball across a net in knock

and counterknock. Deep trees, broad trees,
markers at my gate, at the threshold of this house:
in your two mirrors, in your two pairs of hands,

what is passing, from one to the other?

★

One embryo is returned to me
like a toy to a feather bed. I try to find
its one sentence, one line, one word,

but it hides behind the membrane
that cushions its growing curl.
Stay, if you can, I ask it. *In the new spring,*

I will surround you with pansies and tulips
and the blue iris and the sky.
Or do what you must: I am willing to be broken.

Remember the world
needs us to dream it, so dream well, little one,
among the shadows where dreaming begins.

You are my waking
moment, before the imperative returns.
You are every breathing flower.

★

Each day, I watch the trees grow slowly
ever higher, their midriffs filling:
more leaves upon leaves

which ripple like a reed bed
presenting its sheaves of feathers to the wind.
A young thrush practises flying

between window-sill and branch
or bends the long, new flexing shoots
with his weight and I am practising

being me again, as though only by going
further and further into the heart
of the trees, to the dark-green dark

could I be claimed again
as the unborn are, called out from unglimmering
shadow to place

                on the nothingness
an 'O' of breath and then another 'O' and another.

The boat

Through skin, fat and tissue, the zooming in
        and out of focus, the bean-shaped weight
is now very still, now very quiet.

No more effort of the heart's two valves
        which closed and opened like clapping hands
or two arms that, by waving, kept the idea

of this conception above the water-line.

It has succumbed, like an upturned boat
not yet sunk, but full, sodden,
        floating in a halo of debris.

I carried you, fed your corpse at its mooring.

And nothing to mark your passing, little sewn-on verity –
        just the grave I make in my ripeness
        ripening still.

What is it you cannot be born into?
Everywhere, I look for signs
        and see them.

They hang like flags to the mast of this world.

Voyage of the innocents

Now our mothers have torn out their hair
               at the harbour wall
and each of us is alone again in our separate grief
and the sea has replaced the coastline
                     where Athens sprawls
and there is nothing in the world
but the shifting of the sea's weight,
I place my head on that motion,
         swell by heavy swell,
and wait for my last hours to unfold.

The night comes out, impeccable and silent with stars,
         and our ship travels on,
with barely an oar dipping into the deep
so set on its course is the wind.
One lamp illuminates our faces: seven unwed boys
         and seven unwed girls
lying entwined as sea snakes,
         plus a crew of three.

And all of us with a fixed gaze
         for who would want to see what lies
in another's eyes? It is enough to hold these things
in ourselves, let alone double them
         with a mirror's burden.
                     An honour they call it,
who sleep easy and warm in their beds tonight,
to have drawn that lot that put us out on this voyage:
         death to be our husband or wife or lover,
         the one who steals us from the light.

My body heaves up its bile: what is within
            and without is bitter and salt.
I decay like skin ripening under the wind's bite
or a ship's cedar hull slanted across the seabed:
            not even my name remains,
only the endless breathing of the waves
            and an arc of fleshless ribs.

I sink into the sea, into a mirage
that moves beneath sleep:
                              I am neither dreaming
nor settled into oblivion's all-welcoming state.
I see terrors flashing their girths
and sieving teeth,
            before fading again into the shadows
like sails dropped as the wind turns.

In the deep, the water is as black as bull's blood.
In the deep, nothing alive is fearless.

For a moment, I give in to panic, then the sea
pinches me at the waist, making a line
            as between fish and bird.
I see worms of light on the sloping shelf,
                              a blue exhaling sky.
I swim through the dizziness of my ears
            to the surface of flying!
The waves are the rushing movements of my mind.

            I wake. And must imagine myself again
from the thin rim of my shivering,

for there is Crete rising with the dawn,
its mountains now being born from the horizon.
Soon, the beast will have his unchecked way.
He finds no beginning or end in the darkness,
            only blood, they say, our blood

which changes nothing for us or him
or the weary agony of men:
            the plague, the war, the knife
are still being worked by an invisible fist
and King Minos's grief remains,
            untempered by a stranger's pain.

Later, this ship will return with its black sails
            to the harbour wall where hope has failed.
But I have travelled the illusion which was, briefly, my life.
Now we dock and now the heavy ropes are being slung
from the ship's side. Now I see my foot lifting
and, forever now, it is stepping down
            and stepping down onto foreign soil.

Song

who is the woman
whose washing's in the wind

who stands at the doorway
believing in the wind

as if it were a mystery
which she had seen and named

a mystery slowly filling
each buoyant sheet with sun

the wind is in her sorrow
the wind is in her lungs

who is the woman
who's singing in the wind

the wind that washed her song
lays its breath on her tongue

Venus waking

after Remedios Varo and Paul Delvaux

What unrolls onto the earth's back like a scarf
is silk, the work of mind by mind.

Embroidered onto this fabric is the world,
its seas, flesh and cities in the folds.

Death wants to open me: it draws out
each day into a fine thread of dreams.

But what shall I wait for at the city's gate?
The mountains beyond are stirring: from bones

and silent seas, from dreams settling into stone,
they grow an architecture of the dead.

I frame myself with an anguished skin.
I weave stars along the column of my spine.

Love is an endless generation of feet
on the ground. Nothing is too much for it.

What holds you like a sister
for Jackie

Let us summon the mountains, then,
and throw away the map. Let us have the river
in full flow, falling from its Himalayan heights
and you out again in the curfew, passing
the checkpoint that will cut one life off
from another. Let me be with you this time
at your late-night rendezvous: two friends
to sit at the kerb by the airstrip and wait
for that incoming flight: now negotiating
the mountains snaked into sleep, now heading
over the contours of snow, no silhouette.

There will be a limit to what we imagine
or repeat: so, no fire, no wreckage strewn
like papers from an emptied drawer, no last
thoughts which are not ours to know.
But when your pain builds, layer on layer,
let the clocks wind down in both our minds.
When you gather the tremor and set yourself
like a ruined temple on a hillside, let me not
be absent again. As you vanish into your loss
like one culture subsiding into another,
I will mask myself with stone: we will be

two statues, and into both our hearts let
the fracture deepen and into it both be born.
And when this trick fails, as it will, to find you
below the roofs of Kathmandu at dawn,
grief again will guide you, as it did that night
I would repair, when you were alone

and no one came out of a dark and unlit sky
to meet you for the years ahead.
Poor map that I draw: that rewrites no wrong.
But how constant is grief. Like a sister,
it binds you still, and will not give you up.

At the solstice

Fog hangs on the hillside like an unslept night.
In fields, horses appear and disappear
       like sounds imprisoned in a storm.

The frost crackles gently.

Only half the bulbs in the sky are working
       and even the moon has failed
in its arguments about love.

See how the bareness of the trees
       makes the sky into a broken vase.

★

Come and walk with me in the dark.

The trees are temples in a landscape of doors
and our confinement carries
       a nest of cloud-eggs, a shell of blue daylight
       under our buttoned coats.

We are quite something, you and I,
each with a hand pressed into the same glove
along with all the hope that attends to the season.

The chariot turns the sky a notch towards rising.

The life after

Then what is love, but wildness –

to be like stone, carved by rain,
to be like Lazarus and hear a voice in the dark?

Once more, I go into the courtroom,
       robed in skin.

Again, again, again, I am
       formed in the blue light,
filling the vault

with what I was:
       a gleaming procession of wounds,
       the cloth unwound and winding.

The Black Paintings in Hong Kong

From my refuge in this city of glass,
from its irreligious towers, perpetually lit,
and from the street seller's oil and fizz

and oxtail broth, among the writhing crabs
and the stink of incense and piss,
and the ringing bell, and the escalator chic

– the advert of tiny, adorned feet
and the falling script of wisteria flowers –
it's this horizon I find again: Rothko's

black on grey, his straightness, his pivot
approximated by the eye from a far-less certain
line into his knife-edge, his dissection of sky.

It's his resistance of colour, his moonscapes
repeated at levels of pitch and pain,
the streak of rising white an arrival or departure

in, or from, a place of ash and dust and shadow
that I find again, by the harbour
where the ships dock and the ferry shudders,

and by our window where I watch the planes land.
Not because there is no colour here,
but because there is and because the paintings

hang on a wall that bears out to the brown water
and the line of crystal towers and the Bank of China
in a rolled-out canvas: Rothko, Rothko,

unbearable absence, the sullen moon,
then wild towers, a wildness of mind,
the swirling waters and the deep harbour

and just before that, the red, red
of his last painting which opens up from the anguish
that tore the darkness at Rothko's wrist

and here is opened again, the anguish
I've brought with me like a hymn book,
like the hum of my phone – *turn it off!*

my god, the silence when the breath stalls
for a moment in the body's shrine-like dark –
and it comes to me, after these nightscapes

of absent stars: the total craft of his red
framed mid-vision with this wound
where the canvas appears like sunlight through clouds,

this horizon from which the towers grow
and awe each other with flattering
reflections, this one's glass in this other's,

so all is shimmer and shatter in a soundless,
actionless shatter above the busy street:
I would stand under it as though it were rain.

I would stand under it as though it were
          this boiling rain.

Goodnight in Bethnal Green

It was after they'd unblocked you
like a drain and I'd got over feeling
homeless in the hospital light, after
they'd stopped that heparin-thinning
of your blood and the clot's borders
dissolved as if from an outdated map,
after your heart's vessel had spidered
on the X-ray and was invisible again
with its scaffold of stainless steel, after
I'd fed you soup and kissed the stubble
on your cheek and dared to speak those words
the inefficiencies of love withhold,
after the machine had echoed the pulse
of your heartbeat's tether to the world
and I'd remembered the song you played
to send me to my summer's sleep, no absence
in that still-bright hour, just a little
faltering of your fingers at the keys,
that I stood on those three words of love
again like a bare-skinned child, my shadow
behind me as long as an island. My father,
do you hear the rhythm of the rain?
Fearlessly it falls, saying, lightly now,
sleep well, quietly now, *sleep well*,
until soon the whole deep night
softens and fades, softens and fades.

St Elmo's fire

As the charge from storm to mast
consummates its stress in fire,
           so my mouth sings the lines of your body

and on that bridge of skin conceives
our connection, our *corpo santo*,
           through the sign of a kiss.

As hydrogen with hydrogen
takes oxygen's hand in its own
           and shapes from those courtesies

the soft machines of clouds,
the bolts of summer rain, let's make again
           a sacredness from the bared world:

the candles there are lit
like the spears of Caesar's legion, luminous
           on the ramparts of the night.

Notes

'As flamingos at the water's edge' – Malcolm Lowry's poem 'Delirium in Vera Cruz' begins: 'Where has the tenderness gone, he asked the mirror'.

'Can I only tell you about the rain?' – the epigraph is from Michael Donaghy's poem 'Regarding our late correspondence'.

'The orchard' – the epigraph is from Lorca's poem 'Adam'.

'Bluebells' – the epigraph is from Rilke's poem 'Orpheus. Eurydice. Hermes'.

'A summer diary' – the epigraph is from Lorca's poem 'Song of the barren orange tree' and 'You are my one sentence, one line, one word/that defends my obstinate centre from fear' is from Elaine Feinstein's 'Muse'.

'Venus waking' – the specific paintings are: 'Sleeping Venus' by Paul Delvaux and 'Embroidering Earth's Mantle' by Remedios Varo.

Acknowledgements

Acknowledgements are due to the editors of the following publications in which some of these poems, or earlier versions, have appeared: *Agenda* broadsheets, *Asia Literary Review*, *I am twenty people!* (Enitharmon, 2007), *Kent and Sussex Poetry Society Folio 2012*, *Long Poem Magazine*, *Lung Jazz: Young British Poets for Oxfam* (Cinnamon Press/Eyewear Publishing, 2012), *Mslexia*, *The Oxford Magazine*, *Oxford Poets Anthology 2007* (OxfordPoets/ Carcanet, 2007), *Oxford Today*, *Peloton* (Templar, 2013), *Poetry London*, *Poetry Review*, *Real Fits Journal*, *This Little Stretch of Life* (Hearing Eye, 2006), *Scintilla*, *Stand*.

I am grateful to the New Writing Partnership for financial support. 'What holds you like a sister' and 'Venus waking' were first published on the New Writing Partnership website.

Thanks are due to Mimi Khalvati and Don Paterson for providing an education in poetry, as well as editorial guidance. Thanks also to Selima Hill, Pascale Petit and Todd Swift for their comments, to Aviva Dautch, Sharon Morris, Meryl Pugh and Saradha Soobrayen for their close reading and encouragement and to Philip Borg for giving me the most precious resource: time.

⌐□□ **EYEWEAR** PUBLISHING